MY DAY WITH ABE LINCOLN

Jonathan W. White

Illustrated by Madeline Renaux

REEDY PRESS

Reedy Press
PO Box 5131
St. Louis, MO 63139, USA
www.reedypress.com

Library of Congress Control Number: 2023952363

ISBN: 9781681065069

Printed in the United States of America
24 25 26 27 28   5 4 3 2 1

A NOTE FROM CHARLOTTE AND CLARA

Dear Reader,

The story you are about to read is true. We weren't with Lucy when she traveled back in time, but after she came back to the present, she told us all about what it was like to meet Abe Lincoln when he was a kid. We had our dad write down everything she said so that we could share it with you. The things that Lucy learned about Abe and his family during her adventure really happened! (Our dad writes a lot of history books for old people, and he told us so.)

We hope that you enjoy going back in time with our friend Lucy. She is SO LUCKY that she got to meet America's greatest president before he became a hero. We think you'll like meeting him, too!

Your friends,
Charlotte and Clara

TABLE OF CONTENTS

CHAPTER ONE

FREDDIE'S MAGIC HAT

"It's time to get out of bed, Lucy," Dad said as he turned on the lights.

"I don't want to. I hate school. It's so boring."

Lucy yanked her covers over her head and made a grunting sound.

"We go through this every Monday morning," said Dad. "Come on! It's time to get up."

"No! You can't make me!"

Lucy peeked out from under her covers and saw him walking toward her with a serious look on his face. Before she knew what was happening, he pulled the comforter and sheet down below her feet. "It's cold, Dad," Lucy said, shivering.

"That was so mean!"

Dad turned and walked out of the room. "I'm running late, Lucy," he said. "I have to get ready for work."

Lucy huffed out of bed and stomped in circles around her room. "I don't want to go to school," she muttered to herself. Then she had what she thought was a brilliant idea. "I know! I'll dress in such a crazy outfit that they won't let me go to school!"

Lucy went to her dresser and pulled out the silliest clothes she could find. She grabbed her rainbow striped tights with a hole in the left knee. Then she dug deep in another drawer until she found her green skirt and blue polka dot scarf. To finish the ensemble, she went to her closet and reached up to the top shelf for her pink t-shirt with a smiley unicorn on it. Nothing matched, and she knew she looked *just right*.

Lucy slid over to the bathroom to brush her teeth and put her hair in pigtails, gliding like an ice skater in her tights on the hardwood floor.

"Mom," Lucy shouted down from the top of the stairs. "I think I'm sick." She started talking like she had a frog in her throat. "I shouldn't go to school today. I don't want to spread any germs."

"Lucy Marie Millaway!" shouted her mother, "You get down here right now!"

Lucy stomped her foot loud enough for the whole house to hear. "Fine!"

Lucy moped down the steps, wishing she was back in bed, or watching TV, or doing *anything* but get ready for school. As she slid from step to step, she mumbled something about school and homework and not having enough sharpened pencils in her pencil box. But by the time she reached the bottom of the stairs, Lucy had another idea. "I know," she said to herself. "I'll borrow the top hat from Freddie's new magic set. He won't mind. That will go great with my outfit!"

Lucy's younger brother Freddie had just gotten a magic kit for his birthday and it included a special top hat that could collapse almost as flat

as a pancake. It also had a secret compartment for hiding a stuffed rabbit. Tiptoeing quietly so her mother wouldn't hear her, Lucy snuck over to the dress-up bin. Sitting right on top of the pile of costumes, fairy wings, and princess dresses was Freddie's new black hat. As she picked it up, her eyes gleamed. "Abracadabra," she said as she gave it a little shake. She slowly lifted it up and placed it on her head. Just as it settled onto her messy hair, a bright red light flashed in front of her face, and a strong wind blew in a circle around her. Lucy gasped and closed her eyes tightly, not sure what was happening. The wind blew round and round until she tumbled to the floor.

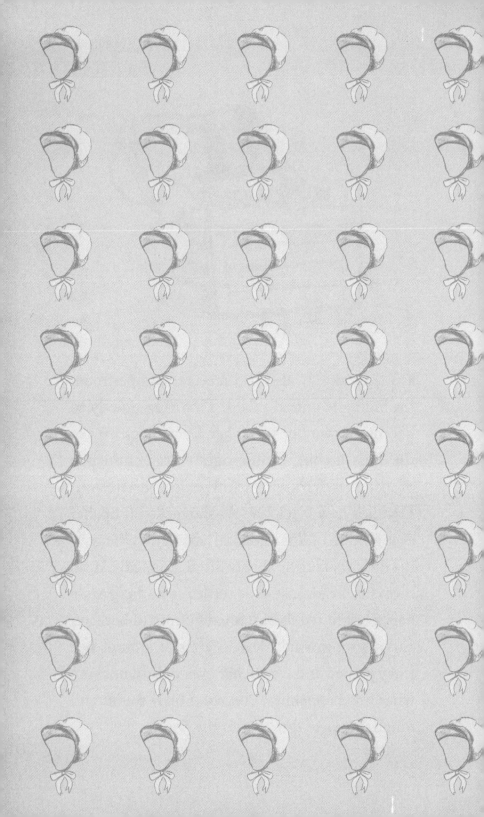

CHAPTER TWO

ABE
AND SARAH

Lucy opened her eyes and looked around, confused. She wasn't on the floor in her family's living room. She was in the woods, lying on a dirt path!

Trees towered above her, and a cool breeze rustled the autumn leaves. She had no idea where she was or how she'd gotten outside. She should have been worried about being late for school, but she was too startled to even think about eating breakfast or catching the bus. "Where am I?" she whispered to herself. "It's like an enchanted forest."

Lucy sat up and looked around. Squinting, she saw a boy and girl walking her way. She could hear the boy whistling a vaguely familiar tune. Maybe it was "Yankee Doodle," but she wasn't sure. Still a little dizzy, she quickly scrambled to her feet as they approached.

"Who are you?" asked the boy. He had a twangy accent. "And *what* are you *wearing*? That's the strangest getup I've ever seen! Did you just come here from the circus?" The boy was so confused by her outfit that he didn't even think to ask how she'd gotten onto the path in the middle of the woods.

Lucy looked down at herself. She *did* look silly. But who was he to talk? He was dressed funny too. He was wearing a coonskin cap, and his pants were way too short. They looked like they were made from deerskin, and she could see his bare ankles!

"My name is Lucy," she murmured. "Um. . . . Where am I?"

"You're in Spencer County, Indiana," replied the boy. "That's Little Pigeon Creek over yonder. Are you lost?"

"I guess so," said Lucy. "I'm not sure how I got here."

"Well, we are on our way to school," said the girl in a friendly voice. "Do you want to come with us?"

Lucy nodded. She didn't know what else to do. She'd never heard of Spencer County, Indiana, before. She wasn't even sure she could find Indiana on a map.

"I'm Sarah," said the girl. "And this is my *little* brother Abe." Sarah smiled as she said the word "little" since she was older than Abe but much shorter. Sarah was pretty and tan, with big brown eyes and curly brown hair.

"Don't let Abe give you a hard time about your clothes," Sarah continued. "I like the cute horse on your shirt. I've never seen one that color."

Abe rolled his eyes, but that didn't stop Sarah. "On his first day of school back when we lived in Kentucky, Abe wore a shirt made out of scratchy wool . . . and a sunbonnet!"

"I didn't dress myself like that," interjected Abe.

"I know," said Sarah. "Mother dressed you."

15

Abe thought back to that day. His classmates had all teased him so much that he cried when he got back home.

"Mother felt bad," Sarah continued. "That's why she made you a straw hat to wear the next day." Abe and Sarah missed their mother. She had died a few years earlier, when Abe was only nine.

"I looked very manly in my straw hat," Abe said. "But *that* is a mighty fine hat," he continued, pointing at Lucy's top hat. "I've never

seen anything like it. It looks like a stovepipe."

Lucy smiled. She straightened her skirt and wiped the dirt off her tights. Abe reached out and shook Lucy's hand. "Well, it's nice to meet you," he said. "I reckon we better get moving or we're going to be late for school."

The three children started walking down the path. Abe carried a book in his right hand, and he occasionally glanced down at it as they went. Lucy's head was still spinning, and the rocks under her feet poked right through her tights. She wished she'd remembered to put on her shoes this morning.

CHAPTER THREE

MR. CRAWFORD

The schoolhouse was a one-room log cabin
with a low ceiling and split logs for a floor.
Instead of glass, the windows were made of old
copybook paper that had been covered with
grease to help let the light in. When
Lucy, Sarah, and Abe arrived, the
other children were just taking
their seats. There were kids
of all ages, from five to
seventeen. They all wore
rough and raggedy clothes.
Some boys were dressed
in flannel, while others

21

had buckskins on, like Abe. The girls wore plain, homemade dresses with simple patterns. Half of the kids had bare feet. Lucy looked down at the colorful unicorn on her shirt and her wacky skirt, leggings, and scarf. She shook her head as she tried to remember what could have made her think this outfit was a good idea.

"Good morning, Mr. Lincoln," said the teacher to Abe. "Good morning, Miss Lincoln," he then said to Sarah.

Sarah and Abe both nodded their heads and smiled.

At that moment, Lucy gasped. *Mr. Lincoln?* she thought to herself. *Mr. Lincoln!!!* For the first time, Lucy realized who she was with, and when this must be. This was Abraham Lincoln when he was a boy, probably in the early 1820s. *She was at school with Abraham Lincoln!!*

Lucy turned pale and leaned forward, breathing heavily and putting her hands on her knees. She was so distracted by the thought that she was with Abraham Lincoln that she didn't realize the teacher was now talking to her.

"Excuse me, are you new?" he asked Lucy. "My name is Andrew Crawford. Have your parents paid your tuition bill?"

Lucy straightened up and looked confused. "Isn't school free?" she asked.

"Oh, no, no, no, my little miss," chuckled the teacher, "but you can stay today and see if you like it." Mr. Crawford then told Lucy to go around the room and introduce herself to each student. "I want all of my students to learn good manners," he said.

23

Lucy walked around the room shaking hands and saying hello. She had never seen a school like this before! All of the children sat in one room together, no matter how old they were. The youngest were at the front of the room, the older kids were toward the back. None of the children had their own desks. They all sat at long tables and on benches that looked rough and uncomfortable. On the far wall she saw a small woodburning stove. The only sources of light were the greasy paper windows, and the only decoration was a black-and-white print of George Washington that hung near the teacher's table. It didn't look anything like her third-grade classroom at school. There were no bulletin boards or brightly colored posters.

Lucy finally found a seat toward the middle of the room, next to Abe and Sarah. She saw little bugs crawling around the bench and table,  and she worried she'd get splinters and bug bites. As she sat down, the bench scratched her leg through her tights. She winced for a moment as she saw the bugs wriggling just a few inches away from her. Then she looked up at Abe.

"We always start our day at school with Tablet Time," she said.

"Yeah, we've got some of those right here," answered Abe. He smiled as he held up a dusty, old piece of slate in a wooden frame and a small fragment of chalk.

"No, no. I mean like iPads and computers."

Abe stared at her blankly.

"Eye patch and con ... poot ... ears?" repeated Sarah with a confused look on her face.

"Yeah, they're like...." Lucy stopped, realizing Abe and Sarah would have no idea what she was talking about. "Oh, never mind."

"I've never heard of those things," said Abe. "I don't think I could see if I had pads on my eyes." Sarah laughed. "But I do practice my writing wherever I can."

"It's true," said Sarah with a funny look on her face. "I've seen him write letters in the dirt and snow! He's even carved some words on tree trunks in the woods by our house, and on the wooden legs of the stools at our table. Father made those stools, so he was mighty angry at Abe for carving on them. We don't have any stores around here to buy new furniture."

Abe looked a little embarrassed. "What?" he said. "I like to learn, so I do anything I can to get better at reading and writing. I don't want to work with my hands like Pa does. When I grow up, I'm going to use my mind."

Suddenly, Mr. Crawford rapped a stick on the desk at the front of the room and called for school to begin. The children all did their lessons out loud. It was very hard to concentrate. Some children were spelling words, while others were reading or doing math problems at the top of their lungs. The littlest children were the loudest. Lucy looked around and tried to copy

what the other kids did, but she got confused with all the noise.

Abe could see that Lucy didn't know what to do, so he handed her a book. "Here, read this," he said. "You can read it quietly to yourself if you want, or you can read it out loud so that everyone hears you." Abe smiled. "I love to read out loud because then I catch the book's ideas with two senses—I *hear* what I read and I *see* it. When my two senses get it I remember and understand it better."

Lucy flipped open the front cover. *The Columbian Orator.* The table of contents had a long list of speeches by people like George Washington. Many were by names she'd never seen before. She tried reading quietly in her head, but the noise in the room was distracting. Slowly and a bit awkwardly, she did what Abe suggested and read the words aloud. She couldn't believe it—it worked! Most of the speeches were too hard for her to understand, but she found a funny poem by Ben Franklin that compared people to different kinds of paper. An infant was like a blank sheet of paper, while politicians were like fools-cap. She read on:

What are our poets, take them as they fall,
Good, bad, rich, poor, much read, not read at all?
Them and their works in the same class you'll find;
They are the mere waste-paper *of mankind.*

Lucy laughed out loud, but nobody heard her over the rest of the noise. She normally didn't like reading poetry, but this was funny. Was Ben Franklin saying that *his* poetry was trash?

After a few more minutes, Mr. Crawford dismissed the students for lunch. The children all stood up from their scratchy benches and went outside into the warm autumn sunlight. The girls talked and giggled near one corner of the schoolhouse, playing games like I-Spy. The boys wrestled and had footraces in a field. Abe was bigger than the other boys and could beat them all.

Lucy had never seen anything like this. There was no swing set, or teeter-totter, or slides. And nobody was playing basketball or kickball. If children wrestled at her school they would be sent straight to the principal's office! But this school didn't even have a principal!

CHAPTER FOUR

THE SPELLING BEE

At the end of the day, Mr. Crawford called for the children to be quiet. "All right, class," he said. "It's time for a spelling bee."

All the older students stood up and went to the front of the room.

"You first, Abe," said the teacher. "Your word is *wizard*."

Abe took a step forward and repeated the word. Then he began,

"W...I...Z...Z...A...R...D."

"Please try again," said Mr. Crawford.

"W...I...Z...Z...A...R...D."

"You just spelled it the same, incorrect way, Abe."

Abe shrugged, thought about it for a moment, and then finally got it right. Only one "z." He breathed a huge sigh of relief.

Mr. Crawford peered over at Lucy with a quizzical look in his eye. "Since you are joining us for class today, you might as well partake in the festivities," he said. "Your word is *butterfly*."

Lucy's heart started pounding so hard that she thought everyone in the schoolhouse could hear it. She knew how to spell *butter*, and she knew how to spell *fly*, but was *butterfly* one word or two? She just wasn't sure. But then she determined that if her *word* was butterfly, then it must be one word.

"Butterfly," she said with a trembling voice. "B-U-T-T-E-R-F-L-Y. Butterfly."

"That is correct," said Mr. Crawford. "Very good."

A few more students took their turns. No one else did very well. By now, Mr. Crawford was getting frustrated. He turned to the class and said, "I have one more word. If it is misspelled, you all will have to spend the night here."

The children gasped as their teacher pointed to their friend Anna Roby. "Your word is *defied*."

Anna nervously stepped forward and started to spell. "D . . . E . . . F . . ." She stopped and started again.

"D . . . E . . . F . . . Y . . . E . . . D."

Mr. Crawford scrunched his nose and coughed into his hand.

"D . . . E . . . F . . . Y . . ."

Poor Anna started to sweat. "Y," she repeated in a low, unsure tone that sounded more like she was asking the question, "Why?" than saying a letter of the alphabet.

Anna didn't know what to do. Then she looked over toward the greasy-paper window and saw Abe standing there, grinning and pointing at his eye. Abe was usually not a very good speller, but somehow he knew this word.

"Oh . . . I," said Anna excitedly, drawing out the sound of the letter for a few seconds. "D-E-F-*I*-E-D, *defied*."

"That is correct!" said Mr. Crawford, relieved that he would not have to spend the night at school with his students. The children all cheered. "Class dismissed!"

CHAPTER FIVE

BACK TO
THE WOODS

After school, Lucy, Sarah and Abe walked a few miles back to the Lincoln cabin. Lucy wished for a school bus or, at least, her shoes. Her feet really hurt.

"Your school is hard," Lucy said to Abe and Sarah. "Do you like it there?"

"Yes," said Abe, "I'll take any opportunity I can to learn. I learn by littles." Abe winked.

"That means a little bit at a time," said Sarah.

Abe continued, "I like Mr. Crawford. He seems very smart, like a wizard." Abe had a mischievous grin on his face. He must have been thinking about how he'd had trouble spelling that word in school.

The three children walked through the woods, talking, laughing, and looking at animals and leaves. It had been a long time since Lucy had gone hiking and she'd forgotten how fun it could be.

"This was a wild region when we first moved here a few years ago, with many bears and other wild animals still in the woods," said Abe. "But now more settlers are coming this way. It's nice to have neighbors and kin nearby."

When they came to a clearing, Lucy saw a wooden structure in the distance. "What's that, over there?" she asked.

"Oh, that's Noah Gordon's gristmill," replied Sarah. "That's where we grind our grain into flour."

"How does it work?" asked Lucy.

"I'll let Abe tell you," said Sarah. "He had quite a mishap there a year or two back."

Abe stopped walking and turned to face the girls. "Well, you hitch up your

horse to the millstone and as she walks around in a circle, she grinds the grain into flour." He took a deep breath. "When I was ten, Pa let me take our horse to the mill. I was glad to do it because it gave me a break from chopping wood and plowing fields. I'm tired of splitting rails with an axe. Father taught me how to work but he never learned me to love it." Abe sighed. "Anyways, at the mill, I guess I got a little too excited and I prodded the horse too strong."

"He hit her with the whip and shouted, 'Get up, you lazy old devil!'" Sarah chimed in, laughing.

"It's true," said Abe looking down at the ground. "Well, the horse didn't like that one bit. She reared up and kicked me in the head and I was apparently killed for a time."

"It was very scary," added Sarah, in a more somber tone. "He was bleeding badly, and I thought he was going to die." A grin then appeared across her face. "But it was funny. When he finally came to, Abe's first words were, 'lazy old devil'! He must have been thinking about that horse the whole time he was passed out!"

"Aw, shucks, Sis," Abe smiled. "Well, I learned to never mistreat an animal ever again after that." Abe looked over at Lucy and kicked a pebble in the dirt.

"That's true," said Sarah. "Abe sure does love animals. Once there were some boys in the neighborhood who were putting hot coals on the backs of turtles to see if they would run faster. The poor creatures. But Abe marched right up to those boys and told them to stop. And they did!"

"Even an ant's life is as sweet to it as ours is to us," said Abe.

"Abe," said Lucy. "Didn't Mr. Crawford say that you have to write a report for him next week? Why don't you write something about caring for animals?"

"Now that's a fine idea, Lucy. I just might do that."

The children began walking again. When they reached Little Pigeon Creek, Sarah's mind took her back to their time in Kentucky. "That horse kick wasn't the only time Abe almost died," she said. "Back in Kentucky, when Abe was seven, he fell into Knob Creek chasing after partridges with his friend Austin."

"How did you know about that?" asked Abe. "Austin swore he'd never tell anyone, and I wouldn't either, because we didn't want to get in trouble."

"Austin told me," said Sarah with a sheepish look on her face. "He said he fished you out with a tree branch."

"That's true," said Abe. "I was crawling across the creek on a fallen tree when I slipped and fell in. I couldn't swim, and the water was eight feet deep. I would have drowned if it wasn't for him." Abe thought for a moment and then added, "I'd rather see Austin Gollaher than anyone else from Kentucky."

Lucy had never heard these stories about Abe. She had no idea that he'd almost died—*twice!!*—when he was so young. She turned to her new friend and said, "I'm glad you survived, Abe."

"Oh, that was a long time ago." Abe smiled and winked. "Besides, I know how to swim now."

CHAPTER SIX

SQUIRREL

A short walk past Little Pigeon Creek, Lucy could see the smoke rising from the Lincolns' chimney. It was a quaint, one-story cabin, about the size of Lucy's living room.

Inside was rustic—a table, some stools and chairs, and a few other pieces of furniture. It smelled smoky from the fireplace. On one wall was a ladder made out of pegs that Abe used for climbing up into the loft where he slept.

Abe and Sarah introduced Lucy to their stepmom, Sally. She was tall, pretty, and talkative, and she moved about the cabin gracefully.

When Lucy first came through the door, Sally stared at her outfit in disbelief, wondering if she was visiting from one of the big cities out East, like New York or Philadelphia.

Lucy sat quietly while Sally asked Abe and Sarah about school. Looking down at her feet, she noticed letters carved on the legs of the stools by their table. "Abe must have done that," she whispered to herself.

"Abe, I want you to go get some water in these buckets," said Sally.

"Yes, Mama."

Abe dutifully obeyed his stepmother. There was no well nearby, so he had to walk about a

mile to get the water. A little housecat went with him, meowing in harmony with Abe's whistling as they went.

Lucy noticed Abe's copybook sitting on the table. She knew she shouldn't open it, but she just couldn't resist. As she flipped through the pages, she saw lots of difficult math problems. Compound multiplication and division, land measures, dry measures, discounts, calculations for interest, and the "double rule of three." She didn't know what any of this meant! As Lucy leafed through the pages, she saw that Abe had also written some funny little poems.

Abraham Lincoln
his hand and pen
he will be good
god knows When

Abraham Lincoln is my nam
And with my pen I wrote the same
I wrote in both hast and speed
and left it here for fools to read

"Abe really is bad at spelling," she whispered to

herself. "*Name* and *haste* both should have an 'e'at the end. And wait a second! Am I the fool left here reading this?"

Lucy was so deep in thought that she was startled when Sally called over to her. "Lucy, would you like to stay for supper?" Sally had such a friendly voice.

"Oh, I couldn't impose," said Lucy. But then she realized that she didn't know where she was, or how she would get home, or when she might get to eat again. "Well," she quickly added, "if you're sure it wouldn't be any trouble."

"Of course not," said Sally. "Tonight, we're having cornbread, milk, and roasted squirrel. It'll be a regular feast."

Squirrel?!!? thought Lucy. But she knew better than to complain, so she said, "Why, thank you, ma'am. That sounds delightful."

CHAPTER SEVEN

MEETING THOMAS LINCOLN

When Abe returned with the pails full of water, Sally looked at him and said, "Thank you, Abe. You are the best boy I ever saw or ever expect to see."

"You're welcome, Mama," Abe replied.

Just then, Abe's father, Thomas, came through the door. "Abe, I want you to stop drawing numbers on the blades of my shovels!" he said gruffly, without looking up from the floor.

"I'm sorry, Pa," replied Abe. "I haven't anywhere else to practice my arithmetic. I'm clear out of paper."

Before Thomas could respond, or ask what was for supper, he looked up and saw Lucy standing nervously by the table. A look of horror quickly spread across his face. "Who's this?!?" he exclaimed in a tone of shock and indignation. In all his life, Thomas Lincoln had never seen anyone dressed in rainbow striped tights, a green skirt, a blue polka dot scarf, and a pink t-shirt with a smiley unicorn on it. He put his hands on his hips and let out a deep sigh.

"This is Lucy," said Sarah in a calming manner. "We met her at school today and invited her to come home with us."

Hearing his daughter's sweet voice, Thomas straightened his shoulders, made his best effort to smile, and stuck out his large, calloused right hand. "How do you do?" he said as nicely as he could.

After shaking Lucy's hand, Thomas looked over and saw Abe holding a book. Thomas thought reading was a waste of time. "Whatcha got there, boy?" he asked as a scowl returned to his face.

Abe sheepishly held up the book. "*The Arabian Tales*," he said. "It's a collection of poetry and stories, like 'Aladdin's Wonderful Lamp.'"

"That book is a pack of lies," Thomas said with a frown.

"Well, Pa, then they are mighty fine lies," said Abe.

Thomas made an audible "Harrumph," threw his hands in the air, and walked back outside to chop some firewood.

"Don't let Pa upset you," Abe whispered to Lucy. "He grew up without education. He can barely sign his name. He just don't understand how wonderful it is to read."

"What kind of books do you like to read?" Lucy asked.

"Mostly history and poetry," said Abe. "I love Parson Weems's *Life of Washington*. I'll never forget the story of George Washington crossing the Delaware River on Christmas Day in 1776. He bravely attacked the Hessians in New Jersey. And he defeated them!" Abe had a proud, satisfied look on his face. But then he began to look more reflective. "The great hardships endured at that time," he muttered. "I cannot imagine." Abe's eyes drifted, as if he was seeing the battles of the American Revolution in his mind, thinking about the great principles those soldiers had fought for. Then he looked back at Lucy. "I also like Shakespeare, but I usually don't read novels," he said. "The things I want to know are in books. My best friend is the person who'll get me a book I ain't read yet."

Abe sat down on a stool and began reading *The Arabian Tales.*

"Abe's read every book in this county for fifty miles around," said Sarah, who was very proud of her brother. "He always has a book in his hand, but sometimes he looks really funny when he reads. On nice days I'll see him lying on his back with his feet up on a tree trunk while he holds a book above his face. As the sun moves through the sky he moves around the tree so that he stays in the shade!" Lucy and Sarah both laughed. "Some neighbors think he's lazy because he reads so much," Sarah whispered so that only

Lucy could hear, "but I know he's going to be a great man someday."

Lucy thought for a moment. "Maybe he'll be president," she said, looking Sarah squarely in the eyes.

Sarah laughed so loudly that Abe looked up from his book, wondering what the girls were whispering about. He stood back up and rejoined the conversation.

"I wish I had a book to give you," said Lucy to Abe, "but I never picked up my backpack this morning."

"Your *what?*" said Sarah and Abe in unison.

Then, Lucy had an idea. "Here, Abe," she said, holding Freddie's top hat. "I think you'd like this."

"Oh, I couldn't," Abe protested. But Lucy insisted.

Abe slowly reached out and took the hat. He flipped it around and looked at the inside. "This has a hidden pocket," he exclaimed with a look of surprise on his face. "I could keep my papers in here."

Just then Sally walked over. "Excuse me, everyone. Supper is ready," she interrupted. "Please gather 'round."

Abe hung his new hat on a peg on the wall, disappointed that he'd not yet had a chance to try it on. Thomas came back into the cabin and the family sat down at the table. Lucy took the stool between Abe and Sarah.

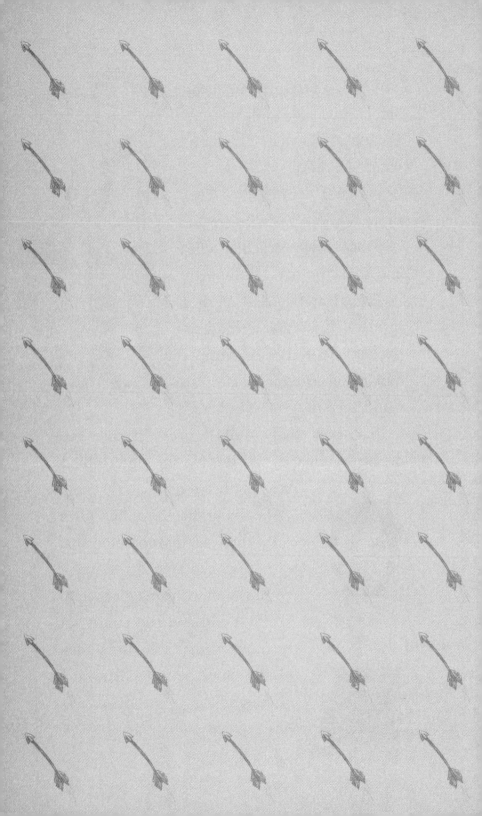

CHAPTER EIGHT

GRANDPA LINCOLN

After dinner—which tasted much better than Lucy expected—everyone went outside to gaze up at the stars. "It's been a long day," said Thomas. "I'm ready to put on my sleeping cap."

"Pa," said Abe. "Tell us the story about Grandpa Lincoln and the Indian."

Thomas paused for a moment. He had been working in the fields all day and was exhausted. But he saw the eager looks on the children's faces. "Well, I suppose we can stay out here for a few more minutes." Thomas listened to the fire crackle and looked intently at the blazing logs, as if the billows of smoke had a mystery to reveal.

"It was 1786, in the month of May," he began. "America was still a new nation." Thomas thought back to that time so long ago—when he was a child, before the United States had a Constitution, or George Washington had even become president. "My father had just moved our family from the Shenandoah Valley of Virginia to the bluegrass hills of Kentucky. His name was Abraham Lincoln. Captain Abraham Lincoln. He had fought in the War for Independence under General Lachlan McIntosh. And when we traveled westward, we went with our famous cousin, Daniel Boone."

Thomas stopped and looked at each child in the eye, one by one. The air was getting cooler, and he took in a deep gulp of the crisp night breeze. He loved telling this story. "We were splitting rails to make a fence in the field of our new farm when a Shawnee warrior came out from the woods and shot my father with his bow and arrow," Thomas said, raising his voice.

Lucy gasped and grabbed Abe's arm. She had no idea where this story was going. Abe looked over at her and smiled warmly. He'd heard his father tell this story a thousand times before.

"He was not killed in battle, but by stealth," Thomas continued. "I was only eight years old. I ran to my father as he lay on the ground, and I pleaded with him not to die. Just then, the Shawnee crept out of the woods and came running in my direction. I don't know if he was going to kill me or kidnap me!" Thomas paused, then opened his dark grey eyes as wide as he could. "With one hand he grabbed me by the seat of my pants. He put his other powerful arm around my neck. And he hoisted me up off the ground and began to run off with me. I thought

I was a goner for sure. But then I heard a loud *crack* and the Native fell to the ground. There, at the window of our cabin stood my brother Mordecai. Fifteen years old, holding a musket, smoke billowing out of the barrel. He saved my life."

Lucy sat there with her mouth wide open.

"I'm so glad that Uncle Mordecai didn't accidentally shoot you, Pa," said Sarah.

"Your Uncle Mord was the best shot I ever knew," replied Thomas. "He said the Indian had a silver half-moon trinket on his chest and when he aimed his rifle he kept his eyes fixed on the silver. Why, he later said to me, 'Thomas, it was the prettiest mark I ever held a rifle on.'"

"You should write that story down, Mr. Lincoln," said Lucy. "It'd be a real page turner."

"What?" said Thomas. "No, I don't know nothin' about writin' or book learnin'."

"Oh," said Lucy, ashamed that she'd made the suggestion.

"Lucy's right," said Abe. "People would want to know this story."

Just then, a loud crack of thunder pealed through the air, and rain began to pour down. The campfire fizzled, releasing a puff of smoke and steam. The Lincolns all ran for cover in the cabin. Abe's long legs got him there first. He grabbed Lucy's hat off the peg and put it on his head to shield his eyes from the rain as he came back out to help the others. As he lifted his hand off the brim, a strong gust of wind blew through the area. Leaves swirled up from the

ground. Lightning flashed so brightly that the cabin seemed to glow. A roll of thunder boomed louder than Lucy had ever heard it in her life. She closed her eyes tightly and screamed.

A moment later, when she opened her eyes, she saw her mom and dad running from the kitchen toward the living room. Dad was carrying a spatula full of scrambled eggs that were splattering all over the floor.

"Lucy, what is it?" said her mother. "What happened?"

Lucy took a deep breath and looked around. She was back at home, in her own time! *I must have come back when Abe put on Freddie's hat*, she thought. *Maybe it was my mission to give it to him!*

"Oh, Mom, it was incredible," started Lucy, talking a mile a minute. "I went to school with Abe and Sarah, and learned from Mr. Crawford, and saw Abe wrestle, and read his poetry. I met his stepmom and his dad. They told the most incredible stories. And I ate a squirrel! It was amazing."

"Whoa, slow down little girl," said Dad. "What are you talking about?"

"Oh, Dad, it was ..." Lucy looked at the clock on the wall. "Oh, no! I'm late for school! I'll tell you all about it when I get home this afternoon."

Lucy jumped up, grabbed her lunch and backpack, and ran out to catch the bus. She didn't even notice that she'd forgotten to put on her shoes.

CHAPTER NINE

BACK TO SCHOOL

The children at school all laughed when they saw Lucy in her crazy outfit and with no shoes, but she didn't mind. She was too excited. And she remembered that the kids at school had teased Abe on his first day, too, when he wore the sunbonnet.

During Tablet Time Lucy asked her teacher, Mrs. Jones, if she could go to the school library to look for a book. Mrs. Jones had a puzzled look on her face. She knew how much Lucy loved Tablet Time. Lucy was equally shocked when Mrs. Jones said, "Sure, why not." Lucy darted

out of her chair and down the hall, slipping and sliding in her tights as she went.

Lucy threw open the library door and shouted, "Mr. Wilson, do we have any books about Abraham Lincoln?" She was panting and out of breath and forgot that you're supposed to whisper in a library.

"Yes, and I could tell you where they are, but it'd be better for you to learn how to find them for yourself," he replied in a kind but firm voice.

Lucy was too inspired to be annoyed. Mr. Wilson took her over to a computer, where they pulled up the library catalog. "Go ahead, Lucy," he began. "Type in 'Abraham Lincoln' and hit 'Search.'" Lucy typed out the words, making sure to spell them correctly. Twelve titles came up. They all had a call number that began with "E457." Lucy grabbed a pencil and slip of paper and wrote that down. She then walked through the aisles until she found the right shelf. She never realized how many history books were in her school's library.

One by one Lucy pulled the books off the shelf until she found a biography called *Lincoln*. She took it over to the large window seat with the fluffy pink and orange pillows and curled up in the sunshine. The front cover featured a painting of a young Abe sitting by a fireplace reading a book. Excited, she opened it up and began to read.

Lucy read about Abe's early years living in log cabins, and how his mother, Nancy, died of "milk sickness" when he was nine years old. Nancy and several other family members got sick when they drank milk from a cow that had eaten a poisonous plant. "How sad," Lucy whispered to herself.

She kept reading.

As a young boy, Abe practiced reading and writing any chance he got. One of his cousins later said he "worked his way by toil: to learn was hard for him, but he worked Slowly, but Surely." To his best friend, Joshua Speed, Abe admitted: "I am slow to learn and slow to forget that which

I have learned. My mind is like a piece of steel, very hard to scratch any thing on it and almost impossible after you get it there to rub it out." Lucy smiled. Now that she knew Abe, she could picture him saying something like that!

By now, Lucy was reading aloud to herself, laying on her back with her feet up against the window, holding the book up above her head— just like Abe used to do on a tree trunk. As the sunlight poured in through the window, she used the book to shade her eyes.

Abe had less than one year of formal schooling in his whole life. Frontier schools like Mr. Crawford's were called "blab schools" since students did all their work out loud. Lucy couldn't imagine Mrs. Jones ever allowing her classroom to get as loud as Mr. Crawford's.

In 1858, Abe described his education with one word: "defective." A year later, he recalled what it had been like to go to school in Indiana: "There were some schools, so called; but no qualification was ever required of a teacher, beyond 'readin, writin, and cipherin,' to the Rule of Three. If a straggler supposed to understand latin, happened to so-journ in the neighborhood, he was looked upon as a wizzard." *Wow!* thought Lucy. *He really didn't know how to spell "wizard"—even when he was running for president!*

Lincoln never hid the fact that he had difficulty with spelling. Once, when he was president, he admitted to a room full of people that he struggled to spell words like "very," "maintenance," and "opportunity." Another time, he asked some visitors at the White House, "How d'ye spell 'missle'? . . . I don't know how to spell it." Lucy thought for a minute. *It's too bad no one in the room thought to point to their eye for the missing letter! Miss-EYE-le!!*

Lucy started to giggle, prompting Mr. Wilson to put his finger over his mouth and make a loud shushing sound. She quieted down and kept reading. Abe was never too proud to ask for help. His best friend as a young man, Joshua Speed, said that he "was never ashamed . . . to admit his ignorance upon any subject, or the meaning of any word no matter how ridiculous it might make him appear."

When the bell rang, Lucy quickly looked down at one more illustration in

the book—a photograph of a top hat with the caption, "As a lawyer and politician, Lincoln liked to keep important documents in his stovepipe hat. Once, he forgot to answer a law client's letter because he left it in an old hat after he bought a new one." Lucy couldn't believe it! *I wonder if he got that idea from the hidden pocket in Freddie's hat!!*

Lucy climbed off the window seat, threw the book into her backpack, and started running down the hallway to Mrs. Jones's classroom. She was so excited to keep reading that she forgot to check it out.

ACKNOWLEDGMENTS

I am grateful to the friends and colleagues who supported this project. Allen Guelzo, Kevin Shortsleeve, Jan Jacobi, and Carolee Dean read the entire manuscript and offered helpful advice, with Kevin and Jan spending several hours discussing the project with me. Jan put me in touch with Josh Stevens of Reedy Press, for which I am very grateful. Josh and his colleagues Claire Nesch and Barbara Northcott offered wonderful ideas for improving the story. Frank Garmon suggested using a hat as a means for time travel. And Michelle Erhardt, Christi Harris, and Alan Skees helped me find Madeline Renaux to illustrate the book. Finally, David Salomon and the Office of Research and Creative Activity at Christopher Newport University graciously funded Madeline's time doing the illustrations through CNU's Summer Scholars program.

Michael Burlingame's magisterial 2-volume *Abraham Lincoln: A Life* (2009) was the basis for most of the research that went into the book. Also essential were Douglas L. Wilson and Rodney O. Davis's *Herndon's Informants: Letters, Interviews, and Statements about Abraham Lincoln* (1998) and the files of the Lincoln Financial Foundation Collection at the Allen County Public Library in Fort Wayne, Indiana.

A curriculum guide for parents and teachers, which includes supplemental information about the history and quotations in this book, is available at jonathanwhite.org and reedypress.com.

Finally, Charlotte and Clara helped develop this story every step of the way. It has been a great joy to work with them, and I look forward to us writing about Lucy's next adventure, which will take her to Washington, D.C., during the Civil War.

– Jonathan W. White
Newport News, Virginia

ABOUT THE AUTHOR AND ILLUSTRATOR

JONATHAN W. WHITE

is professor of American Studies at Christopher Newport University. He is the author or editor of 17 books, including *A House Built By Slaves: African American Visitors to the Lincoln White House*, co-winner of the 2023 Gilder Lehrman Lincoln Prize. He serves as vice chair of The Lincoln Forum, and in 2019 he won the State Council of Higher Education for Virginia's Outstanding Faculty Award.

MADELINE RENAUX

is a recent graduate from Christopher Newport University where she earned her degree in studio art.